CONTENTS

COLOUR FIRST READER books are perfect for
beginner readers. All the text inside this Colour First
Reader book has been checked and approved by a
reading specialist, so it is the ideal size, length and
level for children learning to read.

Series Reading Consultant: Prue Goodwin
Reading and Language Information Centre,
University of Reading

Chapter One

After breakfast, Pete sat in his tree-house, thinking. It was Saturday and, for Pete, Saturday was Mouseday.

At breakfast every Saturday,
regular as clockwork, he asked
his mum and dad if he could
have what he most wanted in
all the world – a white mouse
with pink eyes.

But the answers were always
the same.

"No!" His mother said.
"I'm scared of mice."

"No!" his father said.
"They smell."

"Why can't you get it into your head, Pete," one or other or both of them would say, "that you are not keeping a mouse in this house? Ever!"

So every Saturday, after breakfast, Pete would climb up into his tree-house, thinking . . . *It's no use, they'll never let me, but I'll keep on trying anyway.*

The tree-house was no
beauty. Pete's father had made it
out of odds and ends of timber
and put a tin roof on it. He had
fixed it in a fork of the old apple
tree. It wasn't very big, but it

had a door of sorts, and a kind
of window. Inside there was an
old folding garden-chair for
sitting on, and a shelf for
keeping things on, and the
whole tree-house was rainproof

Most importantly, it was
Pete's, and on its side was
written in big black letters:

On this particular Mouseday,
Pete was thinking about the
actual words his mum or dad
always used. "You are not
keeping a mouse in this house,"
was what they said.

Suddenly he jumped up from
his chair. Through the branches,
he peered out across the lawn.

"OK, so I can't keep a mouse
in *that* house," he said excitedly,
"but what about in *this* house?

Why not keep it here, in my tree-house? They would never know I had a mouse. I could make a nice cage for it and I could smuggle food up to it. We'd have a lovely time together, me and my secret mouse!"

Pete sat down again and took
from the shelf a battered little
booklet. It was called *Mice and
How to Keep Them*. He had

12

bought it secretly a long while ago. He had read it from cover to cover, over and over again. Though he'd never owned one, there wasn't much Pete didn't know about handling and housing and feeding pet mice!

There were pictures of all the many different colours and markings of mice, but the grubbiest page was the one about Pink-Eyed Whites, or P.E.W.s as they were known to proper mice experts.

Pete turned to
the chapter on Housing,
and studied it carefully
for some time. Then he
climbed down the
rope-ladder and went
off to find his father.

"Dad," he said. "Can I make something in your workshop?"

"Depends," Pete's father said. "What d'you want to make?"

"Oh, just something I need for my tree-house. A kind of box."

"To keep something in, d'you mean?"

"Yes," said Pete truthfully.

"All right," his father said. "There are lots of bits of wood there, from that last set of bookshelves I made. I can't help you – I shall be out for the rest of the morning – but mind you don't hit your fingers with the hammer, and don't cut them off with the saw either."

By the end of that morning,
Pete had built a mouse-cage.
Like the tree-house, it was no
beauty, but it was strongly
made. Pete had followed the
instructions in *Mice and How to*

Keep Them. The cage had a wire
top and, inside, an upper storey
reached by a little flight of
stairs: for this upstairs part, or
bedroom, he had made a small,
cosy nest-box.

After a quick check to see that his father wasn't back and his mother wasn't looking, Pete climbed up into his tree-house with his mouse-cage. He proudly placed it ready upon the shelf.

Much of the rest of the day was spent in preparing the other things that would be needed for his mouse.

I must have a tin to store its food in, Pete thought. *I'll need some little bowls for it to eat out of and drink from. But I can't ask Mum — she'll want to know what I want them for.*

Because it was Mouseday and
the bin-men didn't collect till
Monday, the dustbin was full.
Luckily there were some useful
things in it. Pete found a good-
sized old biscuit tin, and also a
couple of little fish-paste jars.
There was a plastic bottle too
– for water – and a large
polythene bag, just right for
keeping sawdust in.

By bedtime, everything was
prepared. The water bottle had
been filled from the garden tap
and the paste pots — thoroughly
washed — stood ready on the
sawdusted floor of the cage.

"Did you make your box?"
Pete's father asked at bedtime.

"Yes."

"I've hardly seen anything of
him," his mother said. "He's been
up and down that old apple tree
all afternoon."

"That old tree-house," his
father said, with a touch of pride
in his voice. "A pretty good
piece of work that, though I say
so myself"

So's my mouse-cage, thought Pete,
though I say so myself. There's only
one thing missing now . . .

Chapter Two

Buying the mouse, Pete thought, should be easy.

First, he already had some money saved up, in a red tin shaped like a pillar-box, which stood on the shelf in the tree-house.

Secondly, the local pet shop was actually on his way to school. Every weekday, Pete and his friend Dave would stop and gaze in at the animals.

Dave will have to know, Pete thought. *I can't keep it a secret from old Dave. And I can't buy the mouse on a Mouseday — Mum and Dad would ask where I was going. I'll have to get it on the way home from school.*

So, as they set out on Monday morning, Pete said to Dave, "I'm going to buy my white mouse today."

"With pink eyes?" Dave said. He knew all about Pete's ambition. "Are your mum and dad going to let you have one at last, then?"

"No. They won't know. It's a secret," said Pete. "I'm going to keep it in my tree-house.'

"That's brilliant!" Dave said.

Pete couldn't wait for school to end. When it did, he and Dave ran all the way to the pet shop. Inside, Pete looked round at the rabbits and the guinea-pigs, the hamsters and the gerbils – until at last he saw in a corner

a large cage with a number of
mice running about inside it.
Some were black, some were
black and white, and some were
gingery. But there was no white
mouse with pink eyes.

"Oh no!" groaned Pete. He
felt so disappointed.

The pet shop man came round the counter.

"What's the matter, sonny?" he said.

"Are these all the mice you've got?" asked Pete.

"Yes. Why?"

"I wanted a P.E.W."

"A pew?" said the pet shop

man. "That's something you sit on in church."

"No," said Pete. "It stands for Pink-Eyed White."

"Is that a fact?" said the pet shop man. "Well, in that case, I think you're in luck. I seem to remember there's one of those left." He opened the lid of the cage.

In one corner was a big nest –
a ball made of shavings and bits
of straw and newspaper. The
man opened it up with a finger.
Inside were some mice. One of
them, Pete saw with a thrill, was
a P.E.W.!

"Did you want a buck or a doe?" the pet shop man asked.

"I don't mind," Pete said, "but I'd sooner have a doe."

The man picked up the white mouse gently, holding it by the root of its tail.

"It *is* your lucky day," he said. "This one's a doe."

"Oh, good!" said Pete. He knew, from *Mice and How to Keep Them*, that it was only the bucks that smelled.

The booklet also said that mice like canary seed, so he bought a packet of that too, and the pet shop man provided a special little cardboard box for Pete to carry the P.E.W. home in.

When they reached Pete's gate, he said to Dave, "Can you go and ring the bell and then, when Mum comes, talk to her for a bit? I don't want her to see me getting up into the tree-house with this lot."

"What shall I talk about?"
said Dave.

"Oh, I don't know. Anything.
Just keep her busy till I get back."

So Dave rang the bell and,
when Pete's mum came to the
front door, he said, "Hello."

"Hello, Dave," said Pete's mum. "Where's Pete?"

"Who?" said Dave.

"Pete."

"Oh, Pete," said Dave.

"Yes. Didn't he walk back from school with you?"

"School?" said Dave.

"Yes."

"Oh," said Dave. "School. Yes. He did."

"Well, where is he?"

"Who?" said Dave.

"Oh, don't start that again," said Pete's mum. "Where is Pete?"

At that moment, Dave saw his
friend running back across the
lawn, making a thumbs-up sign.

"Oh, there's Pete!" said Dave
to Pete's mum. "I've got to go.
Goodbye."

"Where've you been, Pete?"
asked his mother.

"In my tree-house."

"Well, I don't know what's
up with your friend Dave.
He comes and rings the bell
and then talks a lot of rubbish.
I couldn't get any sense out
of him."

"He's like that, old Dave is,"
said Pete. "Can I have a biscuit,
Mum?"

"Can't you wait till tea time?"
"I'm hungry."
"Oh, all right."

When he got back to the tree-house, Pete put his P.E.W. in the mouse-cage. He filled one pot with birdseed and the other with water.

The white mouse hurried around her home, examining everything with twitching whiskers. She climbed the stairs to her bedroom and inspected the bedding in the nest-box.

When she came downstairs
again, Pete offered her a little
bit of biscuit. She took it in her
small pink paws and began to
nibble at it.

You look quite at home already,
Pete thought. *But you need a
name. What shall I call you?*

The white mouse stared, rather short-sightedly, at him out of her large pink eyes.

Some biscuits, like Digestives or Rich Tea, have their names written on them. Pete was just about to eat the rest of this one when he saw the name on it:

"That's it!" Pete said to his P.E.W. "You're Nice!"

Chapter Three

Some days later Pete's mum
said to her husband, "I'm a bit
worried about Pete."

"Why?" asked Pete's dad.

"This week he's spent every
spare minute up that apple tree.
He's got all his toys and books
in his bedroom, yet he's always
in that tree-house. And he talks
to himself up there. I heard
him when I was gardening
yesterday."

"Probably had his friend Dave with him."

"No. I thought that, but I could see Dave over the fence, playing in his own garden. And that's another thing – Dave came to our door last Monday talking a lot of rubbish. And it was just the same with Pete. I heard him saying, 'Nice. Nice. Who's a good Nice?' What sense does that make?"

"I shouldn't worry," Pete's dad said. "He's just playing some game."

"And another thing," said

Pete's mum. "He seems to be eating so much nowadays. He's always asking me for biscuits, and yesterday I caught him with a handful of cornflakes. When he saw me, he stuffed them in his mouth. Dry cornflakes. I ask you!"

Apart from that slip-up, Pete
had managed to smuggle all
sorts of food to Nice. As well as
biscuits and cornflakes, he tried
her with a number of other
foods recommended in *Mice and
How to Keep Them* – bread,
cakecrumbs, and bits of carrot

and apple and banana. He only
gave her very small amounts, of
course, for she was only a very
small animal. But Nice ate
everything he gave her and
seemed, Pete thought,
to be growing
quite fat.
She had
also grown very
tame. Pete would take her out of
her cage and sit in his chair, and
she would climb all over him,
running up his arm and onto his
shoulder and tickling his neck
with her whiskers.

At the end of the next week, Pete and Dave were walking back from school together. It was very windy – a southwesterly gale was forecast – and they battled along with their heads down.

"How's the mouse?" shouted Dave.

"She's fine!" yelled Pete.

"Your mum and dad still haven't found out?"

"No! They never will!"

Later, Pete climbed the rope-ladder to give Nice her supper. The wind was stronger now and the branches of the old apple tree were whipping about. The tree-house creaked a bit in the gathering storm.

Pete lay in bed that Friday
night, listening to the wind
howling outside. For a while he
worried a little bit about Nice, in
her cage in the tree-house in the
apple tree, but then he fell asleep.

Because it was a Mouseday

 morning, he slept
late and, by the
time he woke, the
wind had dropped.
But when he
looked out of his
bedroom window,
it was to see a
terrible sight.

The apple tree had blown
down in the gale!

It lay flat, its roots exposed.
Amidst its broken branches was
the wreckage of his tree-house.

Pete dressed and dashed
downstairs.

"Mum! Dad!" he cried.
"My tree-house is smashed!"

"I know," his mum said.
"I'm so sorry, Pete."

"Good job it happened
at night, otherwise you might
have been in it," his dad said.
"You could have been killed."

Like Nice has been, thought
Pete miserably.

He walked across the lawn and
stood by the fallen tree. The tree-
house had completely
collapsed.

His father came to stand beside him, a bill-hook in his hand.

"What did you have in there, Pete?" he said. "Anything of value?"

"Yes," said Pete. *I don't want to see her dead body*, he thought. *But I can't just leave her there.*

"Let's have a look," said his father.

He chopped away at the tangle of branches until he reached the wreck of the tree-house. He wrenched off the

battered tin roof. Under it was
the garden-chair (smashed),
Pete's pillar-box (bent but with
some coins still rattling in it),
Mice and How to Keep Them (a bit
bedraggled, but still all in one
piece) and . . . the mouse-cage.
By some miracle it seemed to be
undamaged.

"What's this?" Pete's dad said.
"My mouse-cage," said Pete.
"Mouse-cage? But you
haven't got a mouse."

"I have, said Pete. "Or rather, I had. I don't want to see her, Dad. Can you bury her for me, please?"

He turned away.

His father opened the lid of the cage. "Bury her?" he said. "I don't think I'd better, Pete. She seems to be as right as rain." He bent his head and sniffed. "Funny," he said. "She doesn't smell at all."

By the end of that Mouseday, everything had been explained and everything had been arranged.

There could be no rebuilding of the tree-house – and there was no other tree in the garden. Pete was to be allowed to keep his mouse-cage on the workbench in the garage.

"Just so long as I don't have to come anywhere near it," his mother said.

"It doesn't smell," his dad said. "But one mouse is enough, Pete. You're not to go buying any more mice. Promise?"

"I promise," Pete said.

Last thing that Mouseday
evening, Pete went to the garage
to make sure that Nice was
all right.

He opened the cage, expecting
to see her come running downstairs for her supper, but there
was no sign of her. Pete raised
the lid of the little nest-box.

Inside was his P.E.W.

But she was not alone.

With her were six blind, fat,
hairless babies.

"Nice!" said Pete softly. "Oh,
very nice indeed!"

THE END